You Can Call Me QUEEN

Written By: Dr. Jade E Norris

Illustrated By: Arlene N. Grady

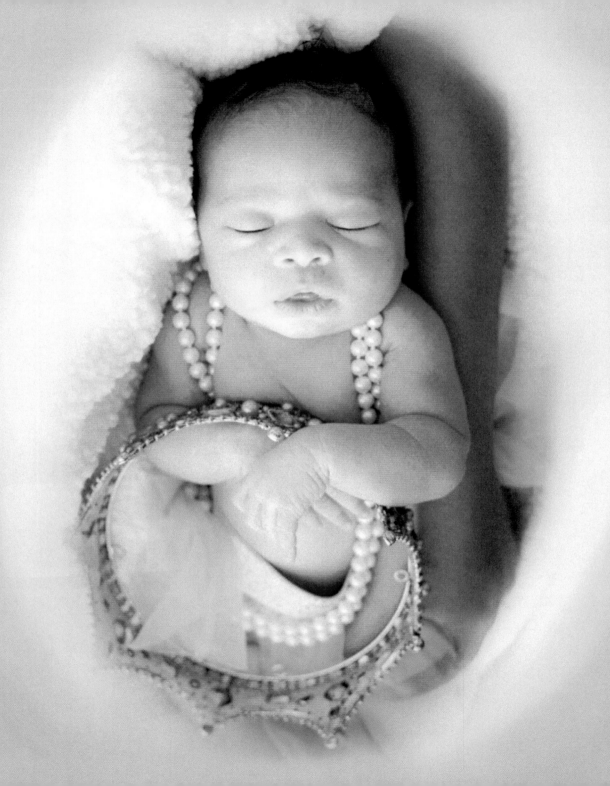

To my Ava Jade, you are my inspiration, my motivation, my blessing straight from God. May you always know your worth and be a light on this Earth. Mommy loves you now and forever.

-JN

To twelve-year-old Zina McMillan, your collaboration on these illustrations meant so much to me. It was an honor to work with such a talented young artist! I can't wait to see where life takes you. Thank you for TEACHING me.

-AG

In all the world there are little girls,
who shine bright like a beam.

They ask my name, I smile and say,
"Well, you can call me QUEEN!"

They say, "Who's that?"
I turn and say,
"Well, you can call me QUEEN!"

A princess is nice,
but please think twice,
yes, you can call me QUEEN!

I'm very smart and very strong,
confidence is key.

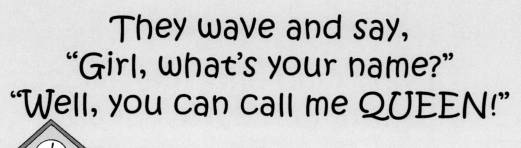

They wave and say,
"Girl, what's your name?"
"Well, you can call me QUEEN!"

I'm very kind and very sweet,
I share and care indeed.

They say,
"Who do you think you are?"
"Well, you can call me QUEEN!"

My dreams are big, my eyes are bright,
I can do all things!

They wonder what to call that girl,
"Well, you can call me QUEEN!"

Made in the USA
Monee, IL
10 September 2020